CARRIE CLIMBS
A MOUNTAIN

Written by
JUNE CREBBIN

Illustrated by
THELMA LAMBERT

WALKER BOOKS
LONDON

For Helen and Robert,
Thomas, Naomi and Andrew

and with special thanks to
Sister Linda King
of Leicester Royal Infirmary

First published 1993 by Walker Books Ltd
87 Vauxhall Walk, London SE11 5HJ

This edition published 1994

2 4 6 8 10 9 7 5 3 1

Text © 1993 June Crebbin
Illustrations © 1993 Thelma Lambert

Printed in England

British Library Cataloguing in Publication Data
A catalogue record for this book is available
from the British Library.
ISBN 0-7445-3192-6

CONTENTS

FIERY DRAGONS
7

MAGIC IN THE AIR
23

THE SPORTS CLUB
41

THE FEELY BAG
57

CLIMBING THE MOUNTAIN
77

"My throat hurts," whispered Carrie.

FIERY DRAGONS

Carrie woke and remembered at once that something nice and something nasty was going to happen that day.

Dad was coming home. That was the something nice. Sometimes his work took him to another country for two or three weeks – and Carrie always missed him. But today he was coming home and she'd be allowed to unpack his suitcase. Inside, hidden among his clothes, would be a present for her.

Then Carrie remembered the something nasty.

Dad was coming home during the

morning, when she'd be at school. Would he remember not to unpack until she was there?

He'd always remembered before. Carrie began to relax. She couldn't think of a time when she hadn't unpacked Dad's suitcase for him.

But then – perhaps all those times hadn't been school days? Perhaps they had been weekend days or holidays, when she was sure to have been at home.

Carrie couldn't bear the thought of it. She would have to stay at home. That was the only way to be sure. But she was only allowed to stay at home if she was poorly.

She got out of bed. She wondered if her throat was sore. It felt a bit sore. She quite often had a bad throat. She went to her mirror to have a look. She couldn't see very much, mostly her teeth, and her tongue, which was huge and got in the way. She squashed it with her finger and was just able to see the back of her throat.

It was pink.

That wasn't the right colour. It should be red. Whenever she had one of her throats, Mum looked inside and said it was "red-raw".

She opened her mouth to have another look. Still pink. Perhaps rosy-pink, but not red.

Carrie got back into bed, picking up Bear from the floor where he had fallen during the night. She lay in bed and cuddled him. Then she held him above her, the way Dad held her baby sister, Amy, high in the air, jiggling her until she screamed with delight.

Carrie jiggled Bear. But her heart wasn't in it and anyway, Bear was not amused. She laid him on the pillow beside her so that his shiny brown eyes were on a level with hers.

"I've got a problem," she said and told him all about it.

Bear looked at her.

"I know," said Carrie. "*I* think Dad will wait for me, too. But I can't be sure."

She took Bear in her arms and looked at the sunshine coming in through the curtains. Where the curtains were slightly apart in the middle, a slice of sunshine fell across her Map of the World on the wall opposite – a river of light going right across the world through some of the countries whose names she knew. Those were the countries Dad had visited. Each had a flag with its name and date – Dad's coming home date. She and Dad had made each flag and stuck it in before every trip. So that she would always know where he was and when he was coming home.

Carrie sighed. She got out of bed, tucked

Bear under her arm and trailed along the landing to Mum's room.

"I don't feel well," she announced at the door. Mum was sitting up in bed reading. She put a finger to her lips and beckoned Carrie over.

Carrie tiptoed across to the bed and got in. On the other side of Mum was Amy, fast asleep with her thumb still in her mouth.

"She's teething again," whispered Mum, putting her book quietly on the bedside table. "I've only just got her off." She put her arm round Carrie. "Now, tell me. What sort of not well?"

"My throat hurts," whispered Carrie.

"Oh dear," said Mum. "I thought we'd left those behind with the winter. Come on, let's go and have a look in the light."

They went into the bathroom. Carrie opened her mouth. "It doesn't look very

11

red," said Mum.

"But I think it feels as though it's going to be," said Carrie. "I'd better stay at home in case, hadn't I?"

"Oh, I don't think so," said Mum. "But, I tell you what, you pop back into bed and just this once I'll bring your breakfast upstairs."

"In your bed?" said Carrie.

"Better not," said Mum. "I don't want to wake Amy. In your bed. I'll bring my breakfast as well – then you and I can have a picnic together."

Carrie enjoyed sharing the picnic breakfast so much she forgot all about her sore throat.

"What have you got on at school today?" asked Mum. "Anything special?"

"Sports," said Carrie, remembering. "Mrs Taylor said to be sure to bring our P.E. kit. It's a special practice for Sports Day."

"You'll like that, won't you?" said Mum.

"Oh, yes," said Carrie. She'd love it. She liked jumping and running. She and her friend David were the best in the class at the three-legged race. They practised every playtime.

"Well, you mustn't miss that," said Mum. "How does your throat feel now?"

"It feels all right," said Carrie. It was true. She felt fine and didn't want to miss Sports practice but...

"Is anything worrying you at all?" said Mum, putting the plates and mugs back on to the tray. "Anything I can help with?"

"Well..." said Carrie.

"Yes?" said Mum

"You know Dad's coming home today..."

"Yes. Would you like him to come and meet you? Is that it?"

"Yes," said Carrie. "But..."

"But?"

13

"Dad won't want to unpack first, will he?"

"He will not," said Mum. "He'll be ready for his lunch and then he'll want a snooze. Besides," she said, picking up the breakfast tray, "doesn't he always need a certain somebody to help him?"

Carried smiled.

"Come on," said Mum. "Time you were up. Don't forget your P.E. kit!"

The sun shone all day. At morning playtime, Carrie and David practised for the three-legged race.

"My dad's coming home today," said Carrie. "He's bringing me a present."

"Why?" said David. He was busy tying the scarf around their legs.

"From China," said Carrie. "It might be a kite. They have bird kites in China."

"Oh," said David. The scarf needed to be just right. Not too tight, not too loose. He stood up. "Right," he said. "That's it. Ready, steady, go."

They set off down the field, moving perfectly in rhythm, as though they were one person instead of two tied together. Mrs Taylor said that was the secret of their success.

In the afternoon, everyone in Carrie's class practised for Sports Day. They stayed outside all afternoon, even for the story, sitting in the shade of the big horse-chestnut tree near their classroom. Carrie could see parents arriving at the school gates. Would Dad be waiting for her?

When school was over, Carrie said goodbye to David and ran down the path. Dad was there. He hugged her tightly.

"Hello," he said. "How are you?"

Carried hugged him back. "I'm all right," she said. "Have you unpacked yet?"

"Not yet," said Dad. "Actually, I was wondering if you knew anyone who could help me."

Carrie laughed. "Me! Me!" she said, jumping up and down.

When they arrived home, Mum and Amy were in the garden. "Hello," said Mum. "I expect you two are off upstairs. I'll bring Amy, shall I?"

Carrie skipped inside. Upstairs, Dad's case lay on the bed unopened. She undid each fastener and unbuckled the straps at the front.

Then she lifted the lid.

It was packed full. On the top were towels. Carrie lifted them out. There was nothing between them or under them. Then she took out a pair of shoes from the side of the case. She examined them carefully. Once Dad had tucked a present inside a shoe. But these

16

shoes had only socks stuffed inside them.

Next she came to shirts. As she lifted each one out, she looked for unusual bumps between the layers. That was always a sure sign of a present. When she came to the last one, one side was suspiciously higher than the other. Carrie lifted it up. Underneath was a parcel.

"That's for Mum," said Dad. "And that one," he said as Carrie found another larger parcel, "is for Amy. Goodness, I hope I've remembered to put one in for you."

Carrie smiled. She'd known her present would be last. Dad always hid hers the deepest. A kite would need to be at the very bottom anyway. It would need to lie flat.

Soon the bed was full of Dad's belongings and the suitcase almost empty. Only a couple of jumpers left. Carrie moved the top one so as to see beneath. There, at last, was

There, at last, was her present.

her present. She lifted it out.

It wasn't a kite. The parcel she held in her hand, beautifully wrapped in red shiny paper, was too soft, too small to be a kite.

Carrie tried to hide her disappointment. She undid the paper and drew out something soft and silky.

"They're pyjamas," said Dad. "Chinese silk pyjamas. Do you like them?"

Carrie looked at them. The trousers were blue like the summer sky. The jacket was blue to match but it was embroidered with tiny red and gold dragons. They pranced across the front and round the sleeves and even along the little stand-up collar.

"I hope they fit," said Dad. "Try them on."

Carrie did. She went to look at herself in the mirror. Proud processions of dragons looked back at her.

"What do you think?" said Dad.

"I think they're beautiful," said Carrie. She flung her arms round his neck. "Thank you."

"Oh," said Dad. "Good. One satisfied customer, then."

Mum thought the present was lovely too. She opened her own and found a pair of slippers embroidered with red and gold threads, but not dragons.

Amy's present was a doll. She grasped it in both hands and shook it. Then she put one of its hands in her mouth and sucked it noisily.

"I think she likes it," said Carrie.

At bedtime, when Dad came in to say good night, Carrie said, "I liked unpacking your case."

"I couldn't manage without you," said Dad, tucking her in. "But you're not wearing your new pyjamas. Don't you like them?"

"Oh, yes," said Carrie. "I love them. But they're much too beautiful to sleep in." She pointed to a hanger on the back of her bedroom door. "I'm going to look at them."

"You're a funny one," said Dad, tucking Bear in beside her. "But I'm glad you like them. Good night. Sleep tight."

"Good night," said Carrie. "I'm glad you're home."

When he had gone, Carrie could still see her present in the shadowy evening light.

"Good night," she said. "Good night, fiery dragons."

*"Oh dear," said Mum. "The sleeves
are far too tight."*

Magic in the Air

Welcome to book week said the notice on Carrie's school door. Every day there were book puzzles and quizzes, competitions and special events.

Carrie loved it all. She enjoyed listening to stories and poems. She had saved up her pocket money to buy a book at the Book Sale. But most of all she was looking forward to Friday.

Friday was Dressing-Up Day, when everyone could come to school dressed as a character from a book. Mrs Taylor said they could stay in their costumes all day, even through dinner time. In the morning there would be a parade in the hall and a competition to guess the names of the characters. Carrie was going to be Alice in Wonderland. David was having problems.

"Has your mum changed her mind?" said Carrie at home-time on Thursday. "Is she going to let you be the Saucepan Man?"

"No," said David. "She still thinks it's too noisy. She says Mrs Taylor won't want me banging and crashing about all day in a pile of saucepans."

Carrie giggled. "Mrs Taylor would have to put her earplugs in!"

Everyone was rushing past them out of school. Carrie and David walked down the path to the school gates.

"But who *are* you going to come as?" said Carrie.

"I wish I knew," said David.

Poor David. It would be dreadful if he were the only person not dressed up. "I hope you will think of someone," Carrie said.

"My mum will," said David. "She promised she'd think of someone today."

Carrie caught sight of Dad waving to her.

"I have to go now," she said. "See you tomorrow – whoever you are!"

She edged her way through the mass of parents, children and pushchairs to where Dad was waiting.

"Dressing-Up Day tomorrow," she said as they set off for home. "I can't wait. Guess who I'm going to be."

"I don't know," said Dad. "Give me some clues."

"I'll be wearing my bridesmaid's dress," said Carrie, "and my hair will be loose so that I can wear an Alice-band..." She paused and looked meaningfully at Dad.

"I get it," he said. "So-called because Alice in Wonderland used to wear one."

25

"Yes!" said Carrie. "Do you think they'll get it tomorrow at school? I'm going to carry a little bottle with DRINK ME on the label."

"Then I definitely think they'll get it," said Dad.

"Good," said Carrie. They turned in at the gate. "Tonight," she said, "Mum's going to get my dress out of the attic and iron it. I'm going to make the DRINK ME label and you can stick it on my little green perfume bottle."

"Thank you," said Dad.

After tea, Mum went up the ladder into the attic. "Can I come?" called Carrie.

"Better not," said Mum. "I'll be down in a minute."

She appeared again almost immediately and came down backwards with a flat square box. "Here it is."

Carrie lifted the blue dress out of the tissue paper. "It'll be just right," said Mum, popping it over Carrie's head, "with your white lacy tights and black patent shoes. What's the matter?"

"It hurts my arms," said Carrie.

"Oh dear," said Mum, standing back to look at her. "The sleeves are far too tight."

"It's all too tight," said Carrie. "I can't breathe properly." She went to look in the mirror. "And it's too short." She was close to tears. "It's all wrong."

"Perhaps I could let it out a bit," said Mum, easing the dress over Carrie's head to look at the seams.

"Can you?" said Carrie. She sat on the bed, shivering.

Mum shook her head. "I'm afraid there isn't any spare material. I'm so sorry, Carrie. I should have realized you'd have grown out of it by now. Pop your jumper and skirt back on and come downstairs. We'll have to think of something else."

"But we haven't got anything else," said Carrie. She thought of David. It would be awful if neither of them was dressed up.

"We'll think of something," said Mum.

While Dad put Amy to bed, Mum and Carrie looked through the dressing-up box.

"What about Red Riding Hood?" said Carrie. "We could make a cape out of a red velvet curtain."

But there was only a pair of blue velvet curtains in the box. And they were old. Everything was old.

"Let's look through your books," said Mum. "They'll give us some ideas. We'll make a list." They wrote down Snow White, the Wicked Witch and the Queen of Hearts. Finding characters was easy – thinking how to dress them was the difficult bit.

When Dad came down he tried to help too. "What about your dressing-up clothes?" he said.

"We've tried that," said Carrie. "They're too old."

She sat on the carpet and opened *Tales from Many Lands*.

"We've thought of lots of characters," said Mum, showing Dad the list. "But we can't think how to dress them."

Carrie turned the pages. She stopped at a picture of a boy wearing trousers the colour of a summer sky. His jacket was blue to match and beautifully embroidered with tiny red and gold dragons. They pranced across the front and round the sleeves and even along the little stand-up collar.

Carrie jumped up in excitement.

"Found something?" said Dad.

"I think so," said Carrie and ran upstairs.

When she came down, she was wearing the blue pyjamas, her present from China.

"Look," she said, "and look at the picture."

Mum and Dad looked. They looked from the picture to Carrie and back to the picture.

"Aladdin!" said Dad. "As I live and breathe. I remember you said those pyjamas were too beautiful to sleep in..."

"But just right for Aladdin." Carrie smiled.

Mum agreed. "You'll need a hat," she said. "Like the one in the picture." She fetched some cardboard and glue and set to work.

"You'll need an enchanted lamp," said Dad, who was on his knees studying the picture.

"No, I won't," said Carrie. "Aladdin

doesn't *have* to have a lamp." She knew there were no enchanted lamps lying around the house.

"Well, we shall see," said Dad.

Carrie went off to have her bath. Afterwards she tried on her costume. Mum plaited her hair and popped on the hat. It fitted perfectly.

"And now," said Dad, "for the thing Aladdin couldn't do without." From behind his back, he produced – a lamp!

It was beautiful, just the right shape and size. Carrie held it carefully.

"Where did you get it?" she said.

Dad parted the silver paper covering, so that Carrie could peep underneath. She giggled. "It's our gravy jug!"

"*Was* our gravy jug," said Dad. "Now it's Aladdin's magic lamp."

"Magic?" said Carrie.

31

There were three Alice in Wonderlands
but no one else was Aladdin.

"Definitely," said Dad. "So just be careful. You never know what might happen."

Carrie was so excited. Everything was coming right again. As she fell asleep, she thought a little of David. But in her dreams she was already Aladdin, polishing the lamp to summon a mighty Genie. "What is your wish, O Master?" said the Genie, bowing low before her. "I am the Slave of the Lamp."

Next morning in the playground, Carrie noticed there were three Alice in Wonderlands but no one else was Aladdin. She looked for David. Witches and fairies, pirates and outlaws, scarecrows and even a lion were swarming about the playground. But David wasn't any of them. He still wasn't there when the bell went and they all had to go inside.

"Goodness!" said Mrs Taylor as everyone came in. "There must be magic in the air. I was expecting my class today but all these people have turned up instead."

They sat on the carpet and tried to make themselves comfortable. But there wasn't as much room as usual. Red Riding Hood sat on a sword by mistake and began to cry. Mrs Taylor comforted her. "I tell you what," she said to everyone, "why don't we put all your special things on this table to keep them safe until it's time for the parade."

So all the swords, bows and arrows, wands, shepherds' crooks, DRINK ME bottles and the magic lamp were put safely in a corner of the classroom.

"That's better," said Mrs Taylor. She began to call the register.

"Rupert Bear?"

"Yes, Mrs Taylor."

"Little Bo Peep? ... The Queen of Hearts? ... Jack Horner?" Everyone answered in their turn. Three people answered to Alice in Wonderland. Carrie remembered to answer to Aladdin but she was thinking about David. She wished he was there. It wasn't the same without him.

"Only one missing," said Mrs Taylor as she closed the register. "What a shame. Never mind. He may turn up later." She gazed around the room. "I wonder," she said, "who can come and show us a bit about their character? Come on, Bo Peep. Come and show us how you lost your sheep."

Bo Peep fetched her crook and stood at the front of the class. She put up her hand to shade her eyes. She looked one way and then the other.

"Lovely," said Mrs Taylor and she began

to sing, "Little Bo Peep has lost her sheep…" and everyone joined in. Bo Peep did some more looking and then sat down while everyone clapped.

Cinderella swept the floor vigorously with her broom. The Mad Hatter and all three Alices sat down to have tea, and the Queen of Hearts strutted up and down with her tray of jam tarts, promising everyone they could have one at playtime. Then Incy Wincy Spider tried to climb up the spout, or at least on to a table and then on to a chair and then on to a cupboard – but the chair wobbled a bit so Mrs Taylor said the sun had come out and it was time for him to come down.

"Well," said Mrs Taylor eventually, looking round. "Who hasn't had a turn? Aladdin? Come on, Aladdin. Come and show us how you polish your magic lamp."

Aladdin fetched the lamp from the table

and stood in front of the class. Everyone watched. Aladdin rubbed the lamp with his sleeve...

The door flew open and in came a Genie! Everyone gasped, even Aladdin.

The Genie was dressed in the richest colours – his crimson waistcoat trimmed with gold, his baggy trousers shining with sequins, and on his head a gold turban with a dazzling jewel at the centre.

"It's magic," said Robin Hood.

And before the Genie could say, "What is your wish, O Master? I am the Slave of the Lamp," everyone clapped and cheered and clapped some more.

"Well," said Mrs Taylor as the Genie and Aladdin sat down together on the carpet. "Now we're *all* here. What a good job Aladdin came to school today. And we've still time for a story before the parade.

The door flew open and in came a Genie!

Whose story shall it be?"

"Aladdin and the Genie!" everyone shouted.

So Mrs Taylor began. "Once upon a time, in a far off city in China, there lived a boy called Aladdin..."

Carrie jumped seven bricks.

THE SPORTS CLUB

One Saturday morning, Carrie was in the garden setting up her Sports Arena. On one side of the lawn was The Jump – a long thin cane balanced on two piles of bricks. Carrie fetched two more bricks from Dad's stack behind the garage and made each pile one brick higher. Then she went over to the hedge to see how it looked.

It looked high. She might need a bit of practice to jump that high. The great thing, Dad said, was to get a good run at it and then tuck your legs right up underneath you.

Next Carrie checked the equipment she used for Aiming – a bucket, a ball and a piece of string. She stepped back from the bucket three big strides. But when she stopped, the bucket looked a long way away. Perhaps her strides had been too big. She started again. One, two, three. That was better. She'd have a good chance of getting the ball in from there. Dad said the great thing was to keep your eye on the top of the bucket and take your time. She laid down the string as a marker and placed the ball ready.

Last of all she set out the plant pots she used for Football. Two big ones for the goalposts and a straight line of smaller ones leading up to them. Dad had shown her how to dribble the ball in and out between the smaller ones, then shoot. Carrie reminded herself not to kick too hard because last time she'd practised, Mum had said if the ball went over the hedge once more, it was to stay there. She was not to keep bothering

Chris and Jean next door asking for it back.

Carrie fetched her football from the garden shed and placed it by the first plant pot.

Everything was ready. The sun was shining. She would start at The Jump.

She jogged across to the starting place, paused, took a deep breath, hurtled across the lawn and jumped. Unfortunately, the cane jumped too – and landed beside her on the soft grass. Still, the rules allowed three goes. On the second go, the cane jumped with her again, but on the third go, it didn't. Carrie sat up to see it safely in place, not even wobbling. She had never done six bricks before.

She moved on to Aiming. She picked up the ball, positioned her foot just behind the piece of string, kept her eye on the top of the bucket and threw. In went the ball first time.

Then she dribbled the football in and out between the small plant pots and shot. Goal! And safely into the hedge – not over. Carrie did a wild victory dance before she fetched the ball and put it ready for the next time round.

She did four rounds, but by the fifth she was bored. It was much more fun when Mum and Dad practised with her.

She went into the kitchen. Dad was pulling on his boiler suit. Amy was pulling a magazine to pieces.

"Would anyone here like to join in Sports Practice?" said Carrie.

"Not me," said Dad. "Sorry. The car is in urgent need of my attention. How about you, Amy?"

"Don't be silly," said Carrie. "Amy's much too little."

"Have you asked Mum?" said Dad.

"No," said Carrie. "Where is she?"

"Next door," said Dad. "She's gone to get Ozzie. Now Ozzie would enjoy Sports Practice. He's a very sporty dog."

Carrie looked at Dad carefully. Sometimes it was difficult to know whether he was teasing or not. He was doing up the buttons on the front of his boiler suit and his head was down, so she couldn't see his eyes.

Ozzie was a very nice dog and Carrie enjoyed having him whenever Chris and Jean went away. But...

"Dogs don't do Sports," she said.

"Oh, yes they do," said Dad. "I knew a dog once that could dribble a football with his nose so fast, he should have played for City Wanderers." He went off to the garage whistling as Mum came in with Ozzie.

Ozzie was always delighted to see Carrie. He jumped up at her, furiously wagging his tail, covering her with extravagant, wet lickings. Carrie was used to him.

"Down, Ozzie," she said firmly. "Get *down*!" And eventually he did.

Carrie turned to Mum. "Will you come and do Sports with me?" she said.

"Wish I could," said Mum, loading the washing machine. "But I've a million things to do this morning."

Carrie looked at Ozzie. "It'll have to be you," she said. "I'll teach you to play football."

"Good idea," said Mum. "But if the ball goes over…"

When Carrie showed Ozzie how to dribble, he picked up the ball in his mouth and ran off. "Come on, then," she said. "I'll teach you how to jump."

But when she took him to The Jump, he went underneath it instead of over. She didn't even bother to show him Aiming. She went inside.

"Ozzie's no good at Sports," she said. "Can I ask David round?"

"Not while we've got Ozzie," said Mum. "Ozzie's quite enough. You could ask David for *next* Saturday."

"David might not be able to come next Saturday," said Carrie.

"Then you could ask Sarah," said Mum. "Or Alison. Or Gareth and Peter. You've got lots of friends."

"Or all of them," said Carrie, sitting up. "I could ask all of them. I could have a Sports Club."

Mum agreed that a Sports Club was a good idea.

"I'll write them a letter," said Carrie. "To tell them what time and everything." She fetched paper and a pencil.

The first letter said:

Dear David,

I am having a Sports Club next Saturday. Please come at 10 o'clock until 12 o'clock. There will be Aiming, Jumping and Football. There will be biscuits and cakes, lemonade and orange juice.

Please reply soon.

Love from Carrie

Mum helped with some of the hard words and then showed her how to put a dotted line and below that: "I can come to your Sports Club. Signed," then another line where David could write his name.

"Then all he has to do," explained Mum, "is cut along the dotted line and give you the reply."

Carrie wrote two more letters during the weekend, one for Alison and one for Sarah. They took a long time and her hand ached from writing. But it was worth it. She put each letter into an envelope and wrote each person's name on the front. There would be plenty of time during the week to finish the others.

Every day that week the sun shone. After school Carrie arranged and re-arranged her Sports Arena. She made three notices – one for AIMING, one for FOOTBALL and one for HIGH JUMP. She practised jumping. She almost forgot the letters.

Mum reminded her. "Don't leave it too late. You need to give them time to reply."

By the end of the week, Carrie had written

to Gareth and Peter and delivered all five letters. Everyone was excited about the Sports Club. Everyone was sure they could come.

"They think it's a great idea," Carrie told Mum. "No one's thought of a Sports Club before."

On Saturday morning, Carrie was up early. She stuck the FOOTBALL notice in the hedge. She tied the AIMING notice round a tree just above the bucket, and the HIGH JUMP notice to a bush close to the jump. She took three bricks off each side of the jump so that it wasn't too high to start with.

Mum helped her set out the biscuits, cakes, lemonade and orange juice on the garden table.

By half past nine everything was ready.

"What are you going to do now?" said Mum.

"Just wait," said Carrie. The sun was shining. She lay on the grass. She didn't want to do any more practising. She wanted to be fit and fresh when everyone arrived. She wondered how many goals they would score. She wondered who would be best at aiming. She hoped she would jump the highest.

Carrie stood up and went into the kitchen.

"What time is it?" she said.

"Five to ten," said Mum.

Nearly time. Carrie went into the front garden to see if she could see anyone. She sat on the gate and swung backwards and forwards.

A black cat crossed the road. Black cats were lucky.

Carrie waited. The gate was warm against her legs. She looked up and then down the road. She went inside and looked at the clock.

"Ten o'clock," she said.

"Only just," said Mum. "Plenty of time yet."

"But it said ten o'clock on the letter," said Carrie.

"How many are coming?" said Mum.

"I'm not sure."

"Well, how many replies did you have?"

"None," said Carrie.

"Oh."

"But they all *said* they were coming," said Carrie, banging out of the kitchen.

She went back to the gate and swung fiercely backwards and forwards. If she closed her eyes and counted ten swings, someone would come. But they didn't. The only person in sight was the postman, delivering further up the road. She counted twenty swings and looked again. Still no one was coming.

She went into the kitchen and slammed

herself down on a chair. "It's not fair," she said. "You try and do things for people and look what happens."

"Never mind," said Mum. "Perhaps they've had to go shopping."

"They could have told me," said Carrie.

There was a loud knock at the front door.

Carrie rushed to open it – but it was only the postman.

"Anyone here by the name of Carrie?" he said.

"That's me," said Carrie.

"Special Delivery," said the postman.

Carrie looked at the paper in his hand. It said, "I can come to your Sports Club" in her own writing and then squeezed in underneath it said, "But I have to go shopping first. See you soon." It was signed "David".

"It's from David," she said.

"That's right," said the postman. "Saw him not half an hour ago. He asked me to give it to you."

"Thank you," said Carrie. "It's about my Sports Club. He can come."

"That's all right then," said the postman. "I don't know." He smiled. "Anyone would think I was a postman!" He went off down the path.

"David's coming! David's coming!" yelled Carrie, dancing into the kitchen, waving the piece of paper.

By half past ten there had been two phone calls. One from Sarah: "I am coming," she said, "but I promised to clean my Dad's car first." And one from Alison: "What time does it start?" she said.

By eleven o'clock everyone had arrived. Gareth and Peter arrived together.

"We're not too late, are we?" said Gareth.

"We had to go to our swimming lesson," said Peter.

"You're just in time," said Carrie. "We're just going to start."

Everyone enjoyed themselves. Alison won the football. Gareth was best at aiming. Carrie jumped seven bricks. She had never done that before.

But Ozzie jumped the highest. He jumped clean over the hedge.

As he landed, Jean's face appeared at the top of the hedge.

"Can I have my dog back, please?" she called.

Carrie lay in bed, cuddling the monkey.

THE FEELY BAG

One evening, when Carrie was helping to wash the dishes, the telephone rang in the hall. Carrie ran to answer it.

"Hello. This is Carrie. Who is it speaking, please?" It was Granny Jo, Carrie told Mum as she came out to join her.

"Hello, Granny Jo. I'm all right," Carrie said. "Are you?"

But it turned out that Granny Jo was not all right. She was going into hospital. That is, said Mum, as they finished the dishes, Granny Jo was fine, but her eyes were poorly. Mum explained everything. For some time now, Granny Jo hadn't been able to see properly. To her, everything looked cloudy and she couldn't manage to read or write.

Carrie felt herself go quiet inside. She couldn't bear to think of Granny Jo not being able to see. Last summer she had stayed with Granny Jo all on her own for two whole weeks. Every day they had gone on expeditions. Every evening they had read stories and played games. They both loved games. Their favourite was I-Spy.

"Could Granny Jo see me?" said Carrie.

"Oh, yes," said Mum, "but not very clearly."

"But she wouldn't be able to play games with me, would she?" said Carrie.

"Not at the moment," said Mum. "That's why she's going into hospital. So that the doctors can make her better."

"Can I take her a present when she's in hospital?" said Carrie. She remembered the time when she'd been in hospital having her tonsils out and how everyone had come to visit her and brought presents. Granny Jo had brought a little cuddly monkey.

"Good idea," said Mum.

That night, Carrie lay in bed, cuddling the monkey. Bear was in bed with her too, but tonight Carrie held the monkey. She tried to think of a really good present she could give Granny Jo. It had to be something special, something that would cheer her up while the doctors were making her eyes better.

In the darkness, Carrie couldn't see the monkey very clearly but she could feel him. She knew every bit of his soft furry body – his ears, his funny little nose, his hands and feet where the stitching was so cleverly done to make his fingers and toes.

She remembered Granny Jo coming to visit her in hospital and saying, "Close your eyes and guess what I've brought you," and placing the monkey in Carrie's hands. And Carrie had guessed. All on her own, without any clues. Like that time at school, when Mrs Taylor had put ten interesting things into a bag and they'd all taken turns at guessing what was inside. They couldn't see the objects. They could only feel them.

A Feely Bag. That was what she could give Granny Jo! First thing tomorrow she would find ten interesting things and ask Mum for a bag to put them in. She could even make some of the things. Granny Jo always liked Carrie's home-made presents.

Next morning, as soon as Carrie woke up, she told Mum her idea. Mum thought it was lovely. And she thought five interesting things would be best because Granny Jo was to be in hospital for five days. She would be able to choose a present every day.

"I'm taking Granny into hospital this afternoon," said Mum. "But I'll be back before teatime. So we'll think of things to go in the Feely Bag then."

"When can I go to the hospital?" said Carrie.

"Tonight if you like," said Mum.

Dad met Carrie out of school. He said Mum had a surprise for her when she got home. She had made a bag just like Carrie's P.E. bag with a draw-string through the top.

"For the Feely Bag," said Mum.

"There's something inside already," said Carrie.

"Can you guess what it is?" said Mum.

Carrie closed her eyes and put her hands into the bag. The object felt like a tin of some kind. One end had a raised-up bit and there Carrie felt tiny holes.

"It's talcum powder!" said Carrie.

"Lily of the Valley," said Mum. "Granny Jo's favourite. I bought it for her birthday but you can have it for your Feely Bag if you like."

"Yes, please," said Carrie. "And I know something else Granny Jo would like." She dashed upstairs to her bedroom. She was sure there was some soap in her dressing-table drawer. Not ordinary soap. Carrie found it and lifted it out. It felt smooth like the one in the bathroom, but it was duck-shaped. Granny Jo would have great fun guessing that. Carrie popped it into the Feely Bag. Now she had two good things. What next? She had to think quickly. They would be leaving for the hospital straight after tea so as not to be too late back.

Sweets. Granny Jo loved sweets. Carrie dashed downstairs. Dad was in the kitchen peeling potatoes. Carrie climbed on to a chair to look in the tin where the sweets were kept.

She was in luck. There were some fruit drops, the sticky sugary kind which Granny Jo loved. Caried loved them too. She counted out five.

"Is five all right?" she asked Dad. "Not for me. For the Feely Bag."

"Yes," said Dad. He looked up. "Is that five presents or one?"

"Just one," said Carrie.

"Then you'll need to put them in something," Dad said. "So that Granny Jo will know."

"I know just the thing," said Carrie. She dashed upstairs and rummaged in her toy cupboard. There it was, the little tin that held her marbles. She tipped out the marbles and popped the fruit drops in. They rattled nicely. Carrie flew downstairs.

"What do you think?" she said, rattling the tin.

Carrie held up the tin and rattled it.

"Sounds great," said Dad.

"Granny Jo might think it's marbles," said Carrie.

"But when she opens it…" said Dad.

"Opens what?" said Mum, coming into the kitchen.

"This," said Carrie. She held up the tin and rattled it.

"Oh, dear," said Mum. "I don't think Granny Jo will like marbles."

Carrie and Dad grinned at each other.

Carrie popped the tin into the Feely Bag.

Three good things. Two to go.

She went back to her toy cupboard. She remembered seeing something when she'd been looking for her tin of marbles. She had won it at her school fair. It had been on one of those stalls where you had to pick a straw and if the number inside was the same as on one of the prizes, you won that particular prize. David had had ten goes and not won anything. But Carrie had won a comb on her very first go.

There it was, underneath some colouring books and a box of crayons. The number was still on it. Carrie peeled it off carefully. The edge of the comb felt smooth and shiny but when she ran her finger and thumb along the teeth, they tickled. She popped the comb into the Feely Bag.

Four good things. Some talcum powder, a special soap, five fruit drops and a brand-new comb. But the last thing must be something she had made. Granny Jo would like that.

A picture.

But she couldn't do a picture. Pictures were for looking at, not feeling. And anyway, a picture would get crumpled and spoilt in the Feely Bag.

Carrie sat on the bed and tried to think of something else. But the picture she wanted to do kept floating into her mind.

A windmill. High on a hill. Where Granny Jo had taken her last summer. Carrie remembered looking up at it, watching the huge sails turning in the wind. She remembered the steep steps leading up to the door, the sky above and white clouds drifting by.

Mum came in with a pile of clean clothes. "Tea's nearly ready," she said.

"But *I'm* not," said Carrie. "I still need one more thing for the Feely Bag."

"What have you put in already?" said Mum, sitting next to her on the bed.

Carrie showed her. "I want the last thing to be something I've made."

"Have you thought of anything?" said Mum.

"Yes," said Carrie. "But it's no good." She told Mum about the picture. "It would get crumpled in the Feely Bag," she finished, "and anyway, Granny Jo wouldn't be able to see it."

"She would," said Mum, "when she's better. It's a lovely idea. It could be a coming-home present."

"But I haven't got enough things to go in the Feely Bag *now*," said Carrie.

Mum stood up. "I'll just put these things in the airing cupboard. Then we'll have a think."

Carrie couldn't think anything except she wished she'd never thought of the picture.

"Now," said Mum, when she came back. "Cheer up. I've thought of something. You *can* do the picture. We can't put it in the Feely Bag, but *in a way* we can..."

Carrie didn't understand. So they took the

68

Feely Bag downstairs and Mum explained her plan. It was such a good one, Carrie felt better immediately.

"So there *will* be five things in the Feely Bag," she said, "but one of them will be a mystery!"

"Exactly," said Mum, popping the last thing in. "Now, we'll have tea and be off."

When they arrived at the hospital, they had to walk along three corridors before they reached the right place. There was Granny Jo, sitting by her bed waiting for them. Suddenly Carrie felt shy. She clutched the Feely Bag tightly in one hand and Bear in the other while Mum fetched some chairs for them to sit on and gave Granny Jo a big hug and a kiss.

"Two visitors," said Granny Jo. "Aren't I lucky?"

"Three," said Carrie, holding up Bear.

She looked at Granny Jo closely. Her eyes looked normal.

"Can you see him?" she said.

"Yes," said Granny Jo. "But not very clearly."

Carrie gave her Bear to hold while she explained about the present. "It's a Feely Bag," she said. She told Granny Jo about the five presents, one for each day, and how she must dip her hands into the bag to feel each one carefully.

"You mustn't lift it out until you've guessed," said Carrie. "Oh, and I nearly forgot. One of them is a mystery! You must leave that one till last."

Granny Jo laughed. "It's all very mysterious," she said. "What a lovely present. Thank you."

When the time came for all the visitors to leave, Carrie gave Granny Jo a big hug and

Granny Jo whispered, "I can't wait to find out what the first present will be!"

Every day Mum told Carrie what Granny Jo had found. The comb was just what she needed because she had forgotten to take hers with her. The talcum powder smelled so lovely and the fruit drops were very refreshing.

All those Granny Jo had guessed. She had needed a bit of help with the soap though. "Because it's a duck!" said Carrie. "But did she like it?"

"Oh, yes," said Mum. "She liked everything."

"Only the mystery present left," said Carrie. "Granny Jo might need a bit of help with that one too!"

"I was thinking about that," said Mum. "As tomorrow's Saturday, would you like to come with me to the hospital? Then you can

*Granny Jo shut her eyes and felt the
last item in the bag.*

help take Granny Jo home afterwards."

"Yes," said Carrie. "I'd like that."

The following afternoon, when they arrived at the hospital, Granny Jo was all ready and waiting. The Feely Bag was on her lap. She gave Carrie a hug. "This is the nicest present I've ever had," she said. "It was such fun guessing each day. But I haven't guessed the last one. I saved it until you came."

"That's the mystery one," said Carrie.

Granny Jo shut her eyes and felt the last item in the bag carefully. "It feels like a shoelace!" she said.

Carrie smiled. "No."

Granny Jo tried again.

"It *is* a mystery," she said. "It feels like a bit of string."

"It is! It is!" said Carrie.

Granny Jo lifted it out and opened her

eyes. "Why, so it is!" she said. "A piece of string. Would you believe it?"

Carrie danced about. "But what do you think it's for?" she said.

"Goodness knows," said Granny Jo. "You'll have to tell me."

So Carrie dipped her hands into Mum's shopping bag and brought out a brown paper parcel.

"It goes with this," she said.

Granny Jo opened the parcel carefully. Inside was Carrie's picture of the windmill, in a beautiful wooden frame. On the back were two little rings, one at each side.

"That's where the string goes," said Carrie. "So that you can hang the picture on your wall. Do you like it?"

She looked at Granny Jo. "Can you see it clearly? Are your eyes better?"

"Oh, yes," said Granny Jo. "I can see

everything. The windmill where we went last summer and the field and the blue sky. You've coloured it beautifully, Carrie."

Mum helped Granny Jo into her coat. Carrie helped put the presents into the Feely Bag. Then they set off for home.

When at last they were settled in Granny Jo's front room having a cup of tea, Granny Jo said, "I-Spy with my little eye, something beginning with G. P. T. P. A. P."

"Oh," said Carrie. "That's much too hard."

But Mum knew. She whispered in Carrie's ear.

"I know!" said Carrie. "Good Place To Put A Picture!"

*Carrie stepped on to the first stone
and stopped.*

CLIMBING THE MOUNTAIN

On Saturday, Carrie was going to climb a mountain.

"Will there be snow?" she asked one morning at breakfast. "Will we need ice-picks?"

"No," said Dad. "It's a green mountain. Covered in grass. We wouldn't be able to climb it if there was snow."

Carrie was disappointed. They weren't going to climb a mountain after all.

"It's just a hill," she told Bear later. "Covered in grass. Mountains have snow."

Bear looked at her.

"I know," said Carrie. "Hills are better than nothing."

She fetched her red woollen hat from the cupboard under the stairs, and a scarf and a pair of gloves. She fetched her *Big Book of Maps* from the living-room. It would be useful to know exactly where they were.

She collected an apple and a banana from the fruit bowl and some newspapers from the kitchen. Newspapers could make a warm blanket.

She would need a flag. She went to the cupboard under the stairs and searched among the buckets and balls and spades for the sandcastle flag. But it had gone missing. So she found a thin stick and a large sheet of white paper to make her own.

All this she took upstairs and packed into her rucksack. There almost wasn't room for Bear.

"That won't do," said Carrie. "Your ears are sticking out. You need a hat. It'll be cold up there."

She borrowed one of Amy's woollen hats. It was a bit big. It almost covered Bear's face. She pulled it up so that he could see.

Every day, Carrie packed and repacked her rucksack. On Thursday, she added a ball of gardening string and a bar of chocolate. She drew and coloured the flag carefully, a range of mountains covered in snow. She coloured it so well, she decided not to take it.

Bear looked at her from the bed. "You're right," said Carrie. "A torch. Good idea, Bear. Torches are always useful."

By bedtime on Friday, Carrie was ready. At the last minute she had eaten the banana but she still had the apple and the chocolate and Mum was going to give her a packet of sandwiches as well.

At last, she climbed into bed. "Don't get too excited," she told Bear as she snuggled down. "Remember, it's just a hill."

But she dreamed of a high white mountain, covered in snow, sparkling in winter sunshine.

On Saturday, everyone was up early and dressed in their warmest clothes. The car journey took a long time. Amy slept most of the way. But Carrie kept her eyes peeled for the first sign of mountain country, just as Dad suggested.

She saw an early-morning milkman and a dog crossing at the traffic lights. She watched houses slipping by, and fields and rivers. And then hills. Hills on every side, rising up into the dark sky.

"Are we there?" said Carrie.

"Almost," said Mum. "Keep watching!" Then she said to Dad, "The sky is full of it."

"Full of what?" said Carrie.

"Snow," said Mum.

"It *is* snowing!" cried Carrie. "Look!"

Large flakes of snow were tumbling out of the sky as if they hadn't a minute to lose. This was mountain country all right, Carrie told Bear. She held him up so that he could see. They were going to climb a white mountain after all.

And then she remembered. "We won't be able to climb the mountain in the snow," she said.

"It may not be much," said Dad. "It may not settle."

But when they pulled into a village half an hour later, the ground was covered in white.

"What about our climb?" said Carrie. They were all standing by the car, looking at the sky.

"Let's give it a try," said Dad. "The snow seems to have stopped. The first part is along the river and then the path goes up through a wood."

81

"Which mountain is ours?" said Carrie, taking her *Big Book of Maps* from her rucksack. "We'll need to know the way."

"We won't need your *Big Book* today," said Dad. "There'll be yellow arrows pointing the way. You'll have to look out for them."

Carrie put the *Book of Maps* away.

She pulled on her walking boots. She sat Bear at the top of her rucksack and lifted it on to her back. Mum lifted Amy into the carrier on Dad's back and all of them set off.

Soon they were leaving the houses behind and Carrie remembered to look for the first arrow. "Where will it be?" she said.

"Could be on a wall, or a tree," suggested Dad.

"Or a gate," said Carrie, running ahead. "Found it!"

Above the gate a signpost with a yellow

82

arrow pointed across a field.

Now Carrie could see their mountain. It was huge. It rose clear up into the sky.

"It's bigger than a house," said Carrie.

"It's bigger than ten houses!" said Dad.

The path across the field led to another gate and another arrow. Carrie was there first. "I can see the river!" she called.

It was fun walking beside the river. The air was crisp and clear. The water was high, rushing and bubbling along over rocks, over stones. She hopped and jumped. She skipped and ran.

"I'm going to climb a high white mountain!" she sang.

"You are if the path's not too slippery," warned Mum.

Where the river curved was a bridge. "Can I cross?" said Carrie. It was a wooden bridge, a plank for your feet and rails at each side to hold on to.

"You can," said Mum. "But we think you'll want to cross further on."

"Why?" said Carrie. She wanted to cross by the bridge. She wanted to stand in the middle and watch the water rushing beneath. "Is there another bridge?" she said.

"Not exactly," said Dad.

"Then I'll just go across this one and come back," said Carrie. "Otherwise I'll miss it."

She started to walk across. She imagined a group of fierce bandits coming towards her. She grasped an imaginary stick and fought them off. "Out of my way!" she cried. "Let me pass!"

Gaining the opposite bank, she saw that Mum and Dad had begun walking on.

"Wait for me!" she yelled. She ran back across the bridge to catch them up.

"Did you win?" said Dad.

"Yes," said Carrie. "Not one of them could stand against my mighty strength."

"I thought so," said Dad.

"Here's your next challenge," said Mum.

Carrie looked ahead. A signpost with a yellow arrow pointed across the river but there was no bridge.

"How do we cross?" she said.

"See those rocks?" said Dad.

"Like huge stones," said Mum.

"Going right across the river," said Dad. "They're stepping-stones. They bridge the river."

"You *step* across the river," said Mum.

"Yahoo!" said Carrie, running ahead. But when she arrived at the stepping-stones, she changed her mind. The stones were huge, as Mum had said, and they looked fairly close together, but between them rushed the river. The river actually rushed over one of the middle ones. And there was nothing to hold on to.

"Who's going first?" said Dad.

"Not me," said Carrie. "It looks dangerous. Couldn't we rope ourselves together? I've brought some very thick string." She took off her rucksack to find it. But Dad shook his head.

"You'll be fine," he said. "Just take your time. Amy and I'll go first. Then you, then Mum."

Carrie put her rucksack back on.

Dad set off. Carrie watched him reach the middle.

"I'll be right behind you," said Mum.

Carrie set off. She stepped on to the first stone and stopped. She took a deep breath and stepped on to the next one. She kept her eyes on the top of each stone and not on the river. She stepped on to the next and the next until she was standing on the same stone as Dad. "Well done," he said.

"This is fun," said Carrie.

"The next one is under water," said Dad. "But only a little. You need to step on and off fairly quickly. But not in a hurry. Do exactly what I do."

Carrie did. "Good," said Dad as she joined him. "Here comes Mum."

"It's follow-my-leader!" said Carrie. She paused for a moment to look at the river. This was better than the bridge. The water swirling by was much closer. "I'm standing in the middle of the river," she thought. And when she reached the opposite bank, she said, "I liked that."

"We thought you might," said Mum.

"But when are we going to climb the mountain?" said Carrie.

"Now," said Dad. "As soon as we enter

the wood. At first the path takes us up through trees."

Carrie picked up the trail again in the wood. It was quiet now, after the rushing river. Not much snow had fallen beneath the trees, though once, where the trees thinned out a little, she said, "It's raining on my nose!"

"It's snowing again," said Dad. "I think it's been snowing for some time but we're sheltered in here."

The path was clear, well-marked, winding on and up. Always up. Sometimes Carrie stopped to look ahead and give her legs a rest. They all stopped for lunch.

"This looks a good place," said Dad.

Next to the path was a rocky outcrop. A pile of rocks fallen higgledy-piggledy made good seats and good resting places for feet and backs.

Mum lifted Amy out of the carrier. Dad

spread their waterproofs on a flattish slab of rock but Carrie climbed up a little way. She lifted Bear out of the rucksack and sat him in a hollow next to her.

Amy was crying. "Is she cold?" said Carrie. "Look, I've brought some newspapers. They would make a warm blanket."

"I think she's more thirsty than cold," said Mum. "She'll be fine when she's had a drink and something to eat."

Carrie stopped tugging at the newspapers, which she'd been trying to pull out of the rucksack. She found her packet of sandwiches instead.

"Cheese or meat?" she asked Bear. "Oh," she said, "looks like egg. Never mind, we both like egg. Egg and cress." After the sandwiches, she found the chocolate and the apple and then she climbed down to Mum to have a drink.

Amy was pleased to see her. She was sitting between Mum and Dad, playing with the car keys. She jingled them at Carrie. She loved to hear their jingly-jangly noise. But when Carrie began her climb back up again, Amy started to follow.

"No, Amy," said Mum, grabbing her from behind. "Climbing is for big girls."

Amy howled. She flailed the air with her fists. The keys, loosed from her grasp, skidded across the rock and disappeared.

Amy yelled. Mum tried to soothe her. Dad tried to reach the keys. Carrie, who had seen it all, watched.

"It's no good," said Dad, kneeling beside the crack where the keys had fallen. "I can get my hand into the crack. I think I can feel them. But I can't see them. It's so dark in there."

"Can't you just lift them out?" said Mum.

90

She held Amy, sobbing, against her shoulder, rocking her backwards and forwards.

"I'm worried I'll knock them further away," said Dad. "If only I could see them."

"Just a minute," said Carrie. Quickly she climbed up the rocks and returned with her rucksack. She dived her hand inside it. "I've brought a torch," she said, fishing it out.

"You've come properly equipped," said Dad. "Shine it into the crack, please." Carrie did. But Dad's hand was too big. It filled the crack, shutting off the light from the torch.

"You try," he said to Carrie. "Your hand won't take up so much room. I'll shine the torch. Can you see them?"

"Yes," said Carrie, leaning over. "They're on a sort of ledge." She reached inside, grasped the keys...

"Careful," said Dad. "Don't drop

them…" Out came the keys, dangling from Carrie's fingers.

"Well done," said Dad, giving her a big hug. He put the keys safely in his pocket. "I think it's time we moved on."

Carrie fetched Bear. Mum lifted Amy, now asleep, into the carrier.

"Are we still going up the mountain?" said Carrie anxiously.

"We are," said Dad and on they went, the path winding ever on and up.

"Not far now," said Dad. "Best foot forward." And just as Carrie was thinking she hadn't got a best foot, both her feet were quite worn out, they came out of the wood into the open. Carrie blinked in the bright light. The snow had stopped. The sun had come out. The top of the mountain was in sight.

Dad went ahead to test the path. "It's

fine," he said. "It's steep but it's slushy more than slippery. Who's going first?"

"I will," said Carrie, her tiredness suddenly forgotten. Up and up she climbed, slipping a little now and then but picking herself up, keeping her eyes on the path in front of her, the sun warm on her back as she climbed.

And then she was there. With Mum and Dad and Amy beside her, Carrie stood on top of the mountain.

Fields stretched into the distance on every side. Farms dotted the hillsides. Far below, in the village where they had started their climb, the golden cockerel on top of the church spire glinted in the sun.

Carrie felt as if the whole world was spread out before her. There was the river and the bridge, the stepping-stones, the wood and the steep path winding up the last

*Carrie felt as if the whole world was
spread out before her.*